Welcome to TRUCKTOWN!

SIMON & SCHUSTER BOOKS FOR YOUNG READERS
An imprint of Simon & Schuster Children's Publishing Division
1230 Avenue of the Americas, New York, New York 10020
Copyright © 2008 by JRS Worldwide, LLC
TRUCKTOWN and JON SCIESZKA'S TRUCKTOWN and design are
trademarks of JRS Worldwide, LLC

Simon & Schuster Books for Young Readers is a trademark
of Simon & Schuster, Inc.
For information about special discounts for bulk
purchases, please contact Simon & Schuster Special Sales
at 1-866-506-1949 or business@simonandschuster.com.
The Simon & Schuster Speakers Bureau can bring authors to your live
event. For more information or to book an event, contact the Simon &
Schuster Speakers Bureau at 1-866-248-3049 or visit our website at
www.simonspeakers.com.
Book design by Dan Potash
The text for this book is set in Truck King.
The illustrations for this book are digitally rendered.
Manufactured in China
0610 SCP
First Simon & Schuster Books for Young Readers
paperback edition August 2010
10 9 8 7 6 5 4 3 2
Library of Congress Cataloging-in-Publication Data
Scieszka, Jon.
[Smash! Crash!]
Welcome to Trucktown / Jon Scieszka ; illustrated by The Design Garage,
David Shannon, Loren Long, David Gordon. – 1st ed.
p. cm. – (Jon Scieszka's Trucktown)
Summary: Best friends Jack Truck and Dump Truck Dan love to smash
things but sometimes their antics get them into trouble until they meet
Wrecking Crane Rosie.
ISBN 978-1-4424-1271-2 (pbk. : alk. paper)
[1. Trucks–Fiction. 2. Best friends–Fiction.
3. Friendship–Fiction.
4. Behavior–Fiction]
I. Design Garage. II. Title.
PZ7.S41267We 2010
[E]–dc22 2010005364
Previously published as
Smash!Crash! by Simon & Schuster Books
for Young Readers

Characters and
environments
developed by the

DESIGN garage

David Shannon · Loren Long · David Gordon

To my pre-K Trucktown pals:
Allie, Angela, Ayinde, Bea, Caleb, Caitlin, Camilla,
Danny, Gregory, Henry, Jasmine, Laura, Lukas, Malcolm,
Martin, Mira, William, Yosef, Amileon, Claire, Conor, Eli,
Gabriela, Gerard, Iman, Julian, Kade, Kennedy, Laura,
Maxine, Michael, Mollie, Roman, Ryan, Ruby, Sofia, and
their wonderful teachers Marie and Rose, Idalis and
Jenny, Meriss and Aida.
—J. S.

ILLUSTRATION CREW

Executive producer

keytoon INC.

in association with
ANIMAGIC S. L.

Creative Supervisor
Sergio Pablos

Drawings by
Juan Pablo Navas

Color by
Isabel Nadal

Art director
Dan Potash

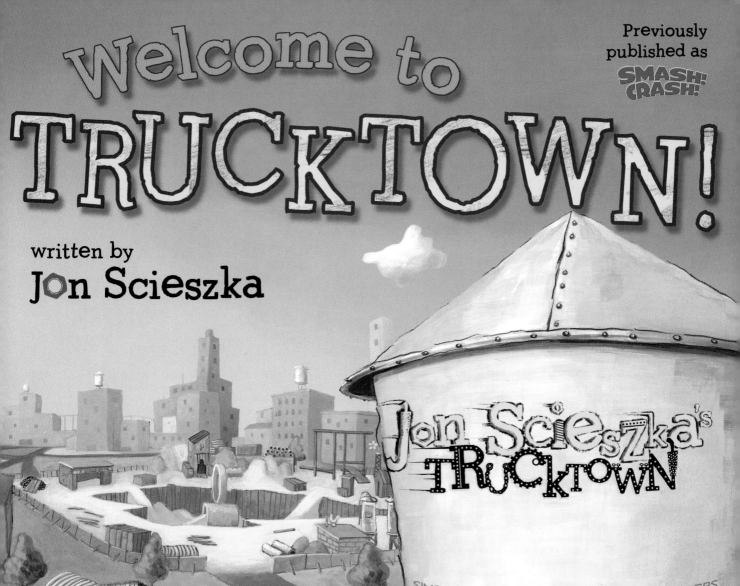

Welcome to TRUCKTOWN!

Previously published as **SMASH! CRASH!**

written by
Jon Scieszka

Jon Scieszka's TRUCKTOWN

SIMON & SCHUSTER BOOKS FOR YOUNG READERS

New York   London   Toronto   Sydney

Jack Truck.

Dump Truck Dan.

Best friends.

Jack and Dan.

"What should we do, Jack?"

"What we always do, Dan...."

A shadow falls.
A big voice calls:

"HEY, YOU
TWO..."

Jack and Dan hit the road.
"Uh-oh."
"Got to go!"

Jack and Dan charge
Cement Mixer Melvin.

"Melvin!" calls Jack. "Time to smash!"
"Melvin!" yells Dan. "Time to crash!"

But Melvin is busy.
"No. I can't get messy.
I'm mixing,
mixing, mixing."

WATER

SAND

CEMENT

CEMENT

Jack signals Dan
and they ...

"You mixed it all," says Melvin.
"You also made a mess."

A clank. A rumble.
It must mean trouble.

"HEY, YOU TWO.
I WANT YOU."

Jack and Dan step on the gas.
"Uh-oh."
"Got to go."

Jack and Dan roll up to Monster Truck Max.
"Hey, Max," says Jack. "Help us smashing!"
"Yeah, Max," says Dan. "Help us crashing!"

But Max is awfully busy.

"Sorry, guys. No can do.
Got to stack these barrels by two."

"Aw, don't be such a
four-wheeler dud,"
says Jack. "Come
on and . . ."

"**WoW,**"
says Max.

"Smacked,
whacked, . . .
and stacked
to the max!"

Suddenly there's a
weird voice calling.
"Oh no," says Jack. "It's—"

"Do you want an ice cream?"

"Do you want an ice cream?"

"Do you want an ice cream?"

"It's Izzy!" says Dan.
"Not now, Izzy," says Jack.
Jack and Dan speed away.

They spot Gabriella Garbage
Truck and Grader Kat.
"Kat and Gabby!" says Jack.
"Smash and crash?" asks Dan.

But the girls are very busy. "My proper name is Gabriella," says Gabby, "and we are playing pirates."

"We'll play too," says Jack. "We are pirates who ..."

SMASH!

CRASH!

SMASH!

CRASH!

"A perfect pirate fort," says Kat.

"Fabulous," says Gabby.

That shadow grows LARGER.
That voice calls LOUDER.

"HEY, YOU TWO.
I WANT
YOU.

I WANT
YOU TO ..."

Jack and Dan try to
race away, but . . .
"Oh no."
"No go."

It's Wrecking Crane Rosie.
Rosie is huge.
Rosie is strong.
Rosie booms,

"FOLLOW ME."

"Where is she taking us?"
"I don't know."

"Are we in trouble?"
"I don't know."

"What will she do to us?"
"I don't know."

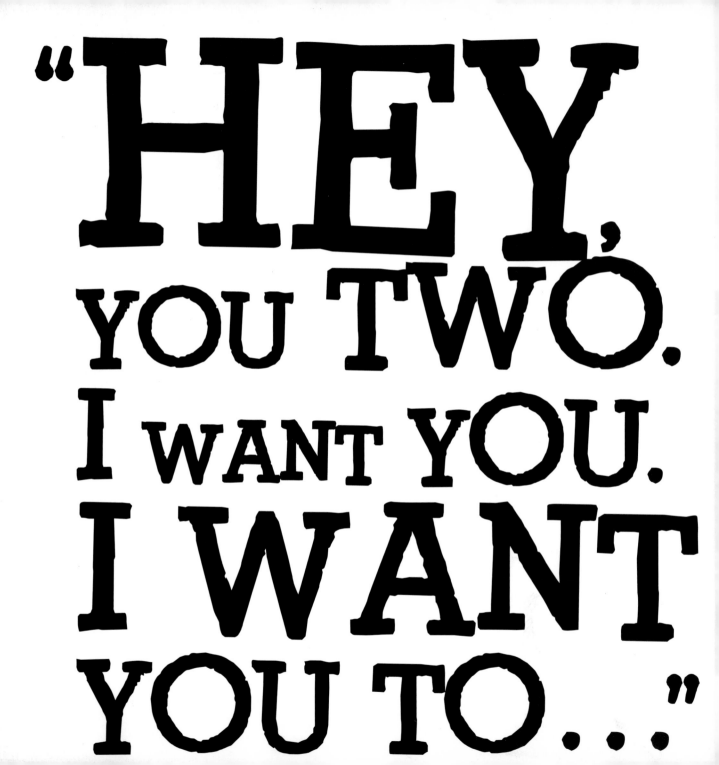

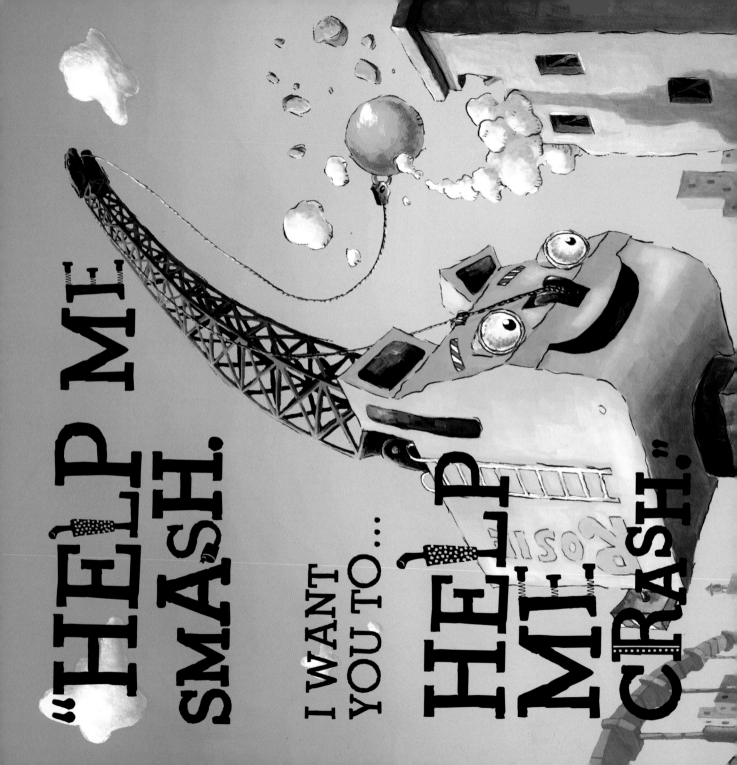

"Ohhhh," says Dan.
"That's what you wanted?"
"We can do that," says Jack.
"We love to . . ."

Gabriella Garbage Truck

Dump Truck Dan

Pumper Pat

Hook and Ladder Lucy

Rescue Rita

Cement Mixer Melvin

Payloader Pete

Big Rig

Grader Kat

Jack Truck

Monster Truck Max

Izzy Ice Cream Truck

Tow Truck Ted